BLUE IS NOT THE WORD
BUCKSKIN TRAIL

Books by John D. Nesbitt

For the Norden Boys
Lonesome Range
Black Hat Butte
Red Wind Crossing
Rancho Alegre
Raven Springs
Coyote Trail
Black Diamond Rendezvous
Man from Wolf River
Not a Rustler
West of Rock River
North of Cheyenne
Poacher's Moon
Adventures of the Ramrod Rider
A Good Man to Have in Camp
Keep the Wind in Your Face
Shadows on the Plain
Field Work
Blue Horse Mesa: Western Stories
Antelope Sky: Stories of the Modern West
Seasons in the Fields: Stories of a Golden West
Blue Is Not the Word / Buckskin Trail

Two Novellas:
"Dead for the Last Time"
"Trouble in the Labor Camp"

BLUE IS NOT THE WORD
BUCKSKIN TRAIL

John D. Nesbitt

SPEAKING VOLUMES, LLC
NAPLES, FLORIDA
2022

BLUE IS NOT THE WORD

BUCKSKIN TRAIL

ISBN 978-1-64540-792-8

For Elaine

Table of Contents

BLUE IS NOT THE WORD

The man and the woman down the bar to my right were drinking light beer in bottles with blue labels. The man was sitting on the other side of the woman, so I did not have a clear view of him. In a small town like Cameron, a person develops a kind of sense for people and vehicles that are not from here. Some of that sense is based on recognition, and some of it is based on surface features like the texture of a person's skin, due to climate, or the tone of dust and dirt on the side of a vehicle. I imagine there are less apparent indications as well, such as how close people stand to one another, how loud they talk, or how they look at one another. I do know that my hunches have been correct most of the time. From where I sat on my stool in the Lariat, I was pretty sure that the woman was from somewhere else. I was sure I had not seen her before. Something about the man, however, seemed familiar.

I did not gaze at them, but when the woman spoke a few words, pushed off her stool, and headed for the restroom, I caught a glance at the man. A wave of dread and dislike washed through me, a sense of something old and antagonistic. What I saw and what I felt happened all at once before I sorted anything out. I kept myself from staring, but I took a second glance. The light from behind the bar cast a dull shine on the man's full head of hair, grainy complexion, and hard features. He did not wear a cap, and although he had not shaved for a day or so, he was what some people would call clean-shaven, as he did not have a mustache or a beard. His short hair was flecked with grey. It had been dark brown when I knew him many years earlier. I was sure that the man who was staring straight ahead and taking a drag on his cigarette was Tragg Tustin.

He did not show any evidence of recognizing me, and I would not have expected him to. He was surly when I knew him before, not only to me but to other men our age. As I recalled, he had been in town for a couple of years. He had his own backhoe and a bobtail dump truck to tow the equipment trailer. The truck and trailer were cream-colored like the white clay that lies beneath the topsoil here. I guess he made good money. Other men said he went out with nicer-looking women than one would expect or that he deserved. I did not keep track of him well enough to know what-all he did, but I knew he gave me trouble over a girl named Lynette.

If I found anything good about seeing him again, it was in recognizing that time had not treated him any better than the rest of us. He did not seem like much of a ladies' man now, but when his female companion came back from the restroom and settled onto her stool next to him, she had an air about her suggesting that he was still the kind of fellow who kept a firm hold on things.

I finished my beer, set my bottle with its red label on the bar, and left. Outside, I gunned up my old GMC and double-clutched to put it into reverse, then drove around the block and headed south out of town. When I passed the last streetlight, I realized that if I had had all my senses about me, I might have noticed a vehicle with plates from somewhere else. But I had been thinking about Lynette, and I still was.

I could always remember the year, 1984, and drop right back into it. I was living by myself in an older rented house, three blocks from downtown and the bars. My wife had left me, and the house had very little furniture. I ate my meals on an old dished-in card table. To keep myself from spending all my time and money in the bars, and to deal with my own desolation, I listened to older music. Of course I listened to things like "Desolation Row" and "Sad-Eyed Lady of the Lowlands," but I spent quite a bit of my time listening to the older country music I had heard when I was growing up. The songs of loss and desperation and guilt had seemed frivolous to me back then, but now, as I linked a more complicated time to an earlier one, they spoke to me. I was like everyone else who had ever felt these songs speak to them. I listened to songs like "Crazy Arms" and "Down to My Last Cigarette" over and over again, along with "He'll Have to Go" and others. In those songs, as in the hollow house where I lived, everything that a person cared about was out there, out of reach, and out of his control. He ran out of cigarettes. He ran out of dimes.

In addition to listening to those songs of heartbreak, I compiled a series of cassette tapes with them and more cheerful tunes like "Wabash Cannonball" and "San Antonio Rose." I alternated sad and happy songs, fast and slow ones, keeping it all older and country. Honky-tonk.

I met Lynette when I was five or six tapes into the collection. She had been in town for a year or so. She was twenty-five, eight years younger than I was, and most of this music was not very familiar to her. She knew the singers who were becoming popular then, like George Strait and Reba McEntire. She got a kick out of some of the older stuff, and we had some good times on the yellow-and-brown shag carpet in my almost-empty living room. She also stayed over a couple of times and had coffee and cereal with me at the wobbly card table.

But all of that came to an end. She had been going out with Tragg Tustin and had broken up with him. She said he told her he wanted her back. He stopped me on the street and told me to stay away from her. I took a line from a song and told him that wishing wouldn't make it so. The next thing I knew, I heard they left town together.

Now, twenty-four years later, I wondered where she had ended up, and like the sentimental fool I had always been, I thought I would like to see her again, if only to find out whatever became of her.

At my home in the country, still feeling the jolt of having seen Tragg Tustin after so many years, I poured a shot of whiskey and put on a new CD by Patty Loveless called *Sleepless Nights*. It had a wistful blue cover and was full of old honky-tonk classics. When it came to "Crazy Arms," I felt transported back to my house in town, where I walked among the sparse rooms, sat on the floor with my back to a bare wall, and thought about lost times. As I listened to the song a couple of more times, I realized that now I was doing something similar, linking the present with a past era.

When the Patty Loveless CD was over, I put on a CD of k.d. lang's *Shadowland*, where I found her version of "Down to My Last Cigarette." Like Patty Loveless, she had a perfect balance between restraint and indulgence. Beautiful sadness. One nice feature of a CD player is that it makes it a great deal easier than on an LP to listen to a song over and over.

I made myself stop listening to that song and went back to earlier songs, now on LP. I listened to "He'll Have to Go" and "Little Old Dime," feeling again how it was to have things out of reach. From there I went back to the CD player and listened to "Send a Message to My Heart" with Patty Loveless and Dwight Yoakam. It was one of the first songs I got stuck on when I bought a CD player, after my second big fall in life, when a woman left me waiting. The song always made me hope I would see her again as well, but the reality was that all I ever did was hope. But it was a good wish-fulfilling song about yearning for one another across time and space. And though I never forgot about the woman who stood me up, the song also made me think, on this evening by myself, about Lynette Cole, some twenty-four years in the past.

* * * * *

Antelope season opened on October 1, which fell on a Wednesday. I had arranged to take the afternoon off, and a friend from work did the same. His name was Allen Woodward. As we rolled out north of town in my old GMC with our rifles in the gun rack, I said, "Did you ever know a guy by the name of Tragg Tustin?"

"Not that I recall. Why?"

"I saw him in town over the weekend. I hadn't seen him for a long time, and now he's back, with some other woman."

"I wouldn't know. When was it you knew him?"

"In 1984."

"I wasn't here then. I was living in Douglas."

"He was in town for a couple of years. He was out in the bars like I was. I had gone through my divorce, and I was living by myself in town. Not a good time. Trying to meet women, and nothing lasting very long."

"I know what it's like."

"I was thirty-three at the time. This guy was about five years younger. We both went out with the same girl. She was about twenty-five. Nice girl. Named Lynette. She'd been in town for about a year. As I understood it, she had been going out with him and had broken up. She was seeing me, and he got jealous and possessive. Then they both left town."

"Together?"

"From what I understood. I never knew what happened to her, but I often wondered."

"Sure."

"And now he comes back, with someone else. Doesn't surprise me that he's not with her, but it makes me wonder all over again about her."

"I imagine. What did you say his name is?"

"Tragg Tustin. He had his own truck and backhoe at the time."

Allen shook his head. "I don't think I've ever heard of him. The name Tragg isn't very common."

"She said it was a nickname he got in high school, after some athlete at the time."

"I don't remember any athlete with that name, but he could have been some local hero where this guy went to school. The only Tragg I remember was a caveman comic book character at about that time, middle or late seventies. For as much as it matters, maybe the athlete got his nickname from the comic book character."

"Who knows. Anyway, I never liked the guy. And now he's got me wondering about whatever happened to Lynette."

"Don't think about it too much. It'll ruin your aim."

"Yeah, I know. Help you get lost in the mountains when you're hunting elk, too. Not to mention that it's not good for your blood pressure, cholesterol, and glucose."

"Don't talk like that. I want to have a beer when we get back to town tonight, and I don't want to feel guilty."

BLUE IS NOT THE WORD

* * * * *

Allen brought down a nice buck antelope at about four in the afternoon. We skinned it and dressed it there on the prairie, and we had it hanging in his garage by seven-thirty. I drank a light beer with him, and to take the taste out of my mouth, I stopped at the Lariat. I drank one beer there. I did not see Tragg Tustin or his companion. I went home and listened to "Crazy Arms" and let myself feel a bit blue about Lynette Cole.

* * * * *

As a general practice at this stage in my life, I did not go to the bars during the week. But seeing my old nemesis had brought my curiosity up, so on Thursday, I stopped in the Lariat to have a single beer. Again, I did not see Tustin. I left downtown, drove south, and stopped at the Buckhorn, a tavern with a gravel parking lot. I went in through the side door, and I was not surprised to see Tustin sitting at the bar with a pack of cigarettes and a bottle of light beer in front of him. He was watching a television above the back of the bar. A woman had her back to him as she washed and rinsed drink glasses.

She must have seen me out of the corner of her eye, for she wiped her hands on a towel and turned around. She was the woman who had been with Tustin a few nights earlier. They seemed at home here.

I ordered a bottle of beer and drank it without a glass. I did not feel rattled in Tustin's presence, but I did not feel comfortable, either. I finished my beer and headed home. Halfway there, I realized that once again I had not noticed an out-of-town vehicle. License plates in Wyoming are identified by a county number to the left of the bronc rider, so a person can identify a vehicle that is from out of town as well as one that is from out of state. I had missed my chance, but now that I knew where to find Tustin and his woman, I could be on the lookout.

As for my own outfit, I assumed that my dark blue GMC with round headlights, a gun rack, and an old aluminum camper shell was in the subconscious inventory of everyone in town. I had been driving it since before my wife left me, and it was on its third engine. It was as typical a vehicle as one would see in the gravel lot at the Buckhorn.

I thought I was a typical patron as well. Tustin had paid me no attention, but I assumed he recognized me. I doubted that he would say anything to his companion, but I thought I might be able to tell if she served me a beer again.

* * * * *

I was driving my pickup in antelope country when the sun came up on Saturday morning. I was used to hunting by myself, and I enjoyed the sky in the east as it turned from scarlet to pink to yellow and then pale blue. Antelope with their white rumps and bellies became more visible as sunlight took over the shadows at ground level. The ranches where I had permission to hunt lay farther north, so I appreciated the quiet and solitude of the dawn as I drove on.

Most pastures in this wide grassland measured a square mile or more. Once I was inside a pasture with the wire gate closed behind me, my method was to follow the two-track trails that ranchers used for checking cattle. The trails led through low, rolling country, often from one windmill to another. If I saw antelope, I tried approaching on foot, using a rise in the ground as cover. Later in the fall, the antelope would gather in herds of a hundred or more, with several as lookouts, and it would be hard to get within half a mile of them. At this point, a fellow could on occasions come within shooting range, which for me was two hundred yards.

It was common to lose sight of roads and fences and to drift along in the tawny sea of grass with a vast sky overhead. I had learned not to be in a hurry, not to take bad shots to begin with, and not to shoot at running animals. One bad shot led to another. I told myself there were always more antelope somewhere.

The sun rose, and the day warmed. Dry particles of grass rose and came in through the window as I puttered along the two-track trails, and dust rose on the unpaved roads as I drove from one pasture to another. Radio reception was poor in this interior country, and I had quit bringing along my own music years earlier. Quietness was better. I knew these plains could be merciless in winter, but on a warm autumn day, a person ambled on and waited to see what would come up.

I had eaten my lunch in a low spot, tucked away out in the middle of a pasture, and I was making my way to my next opportunity. I was driving west on a washboard road toward a more-traveled road that I intended to take to the north. The land rose on my left, so I could not see the main road in that direction, but a low cloud of dust told me to slow down. I rolled up my window and slowed to a crawl as a white Dodge pickup rumbled by. I could not see license plates, but I registered two other features at once. Like other Dodge pickups, this one had areas where the paint had flaked or peeled away and revealed a grey undercoat. Unlike other Dodge pickups, this one was driven by Tragg Tustin.

He seemed intent on the road ahead, as he did not glance at the side road where I now came to a stop some fifty yards away. I did not think he was hunting antelope, as he was not wearing a cap of any kind, and there was no glow of hunter orange from a cap on the dashboard or a vest on the front seat. The pickup was less than ten years old, with an extended cab and big tires, eating up the road at a faster rate than the average antelope hunting outfit.

As I had been planning to turn north, I would now be following him. I knew that in the flatter stretches, a person could see a vehicle two or three miles ahead or behind, but the road north at this point went through quite a few dips, so drivers saw each other only once in a while. I also knew it was possible to drive over a rise and come up on a pickup of antelope hunters glassing a bunch of animals out in a pasture. For all I knew, Tustin could be pulled over as well. It also occurred to me that he could turn around at any point. I did not like the idea of him knowing I was following him, which I knew I was doing at that point. So I took it slow and followed the Dodge pickup at a distance.

The road led to an area I had not hunted for several years, but I remembered the layout and landmarks from having been there many times. I knew there was a main crossroad about ten miles north of where I first saw Tustin drive by. I decided that if he did not turn at the crossroad, I would, and if he did turn, I would drive by. In the meanwhile, I hoped he would not pull over or turn around.

Because of the lay of the land, I had to follow him a little closer to see what he did at the intersection, and when he turned left, I slowed down. Even at that, he had not gone far to the west when I came to the crossroads and drove through. He had either slowed or stopped next to a corrugated metal shed about a quarter of a mile in. He may have stopped, but his brake lights were not lit as I drove past.

The road north at that point became a little narrower, and the hills were closer together, so I slowed down and looked for a spot where I could turn around and have a vantage point. I knew that the road he had taken went west through the same kind of grass country, with very few ranch houses, for several miles until it came to a T. At that point, a person could turn around or drive on even farther until he came to the paved highway going north and south. I decided to wait for twenty minutes.

The time was up, and I was waiting a few minutes more, when a white vehicle appeared about three miles to the west. At that distance, it did not seem to be going very fast, but it grew larger. I lost sight of it when it came close to the metal shed, which was out of my view, and I did not see the white pickup again until it had turned at the intersection and was heading south toward town.

I let out a long, low breath, started my engine, and took my time driving to the crossroads. In the many times I had thought about this area, I always remembered the shed, but I had it closer to the corner. I turned right, drove a quarter of a mile, slowed for a cattle guard, and continued at a slow rate. The shed was as I remembered it, maybe a little larger. It sat on the edge of an unfenced pasture, facing east with its double sliding doors closed. It was about nine feet high on the side walls and four or five feet higher at the peak. I guessed it to be about eighteen feet wide and about thirty feet long, all clad in that bluish-grey corrugated metal that was so common for so many years. It did not seem to have changed since I had seen it last.

I drove on west for a few miles. Past the first ranch house, the cattle guards became narrower, and the road appeared less traveled and less maintained than I remembered it. I saw dried ruts in a couple of low spots where people had gotten stuck in the wet weather of late spring and early summer. The land rose, and I remembered a couple of places on my left where I had gotten antelope, one up against a dirt bank and another near a windmill. The roadside dust lay thick, also as I remembered it, and I came to the T.

I had been looking all along for a place where someone might have turned around, and here I found it. Large tire tracks showed in the dust, and two beer bottles with blue labels lay at the foot of the embankment next to a wet spot where someone had taken a leak.

I finished turning around and headed east again. The sun was behind me now. I took my time, avoiding holes and ruts, slowing for the cattle guards, and keeping an eye out for other vehicles.

When I came to the shed again, I slowed and then parked without making a conscious decision to do so. I got out, and like anyone else in this country, I left the window rolled down, a rifle in the gun rack, and the key in the ignition as I walked across the road.

I saw the wide tracks of the Dodge, the narrower tracks of my GMC, and the older tracks of a deer or antelope. The hoofprints reminded me of a time I saw a large buck deer on the other side of the road, closer to the corner. I walked the length of the building but did not go onto the property itself. At the east end, I observed the double doors, now in shadow, mounted on an overhead track. They were held together by a hasp but no lock. For a second I imagined looking in, but I thought better of it and walked back to my pickup.

I drove south to the area where I had permission, but I no longer felt like hunting. Following the white Dodge had taken the enjoyment out of being on my own under a big sky. I thought it was just as well not to hunt, for as Allen had said, a fellow didn't hunt as well when he had other things on his mind. I did not want to make a bad shot and have to chase a crippled animal at the end of the day.

On my way home, I drove through town, where yellow leaves lay on the front lawns of houses where people had put out flags for Nebraska and the University of Wyoming, who both had games that day.

* * * * *

I was back in the spirit the next day, and I shot an average-sized buck antelope at about ten in the morning. I did a neat job of skinning and dressing the carcass, under a warming sun, in the middle of the sea of grass with no road or fence in sight.

* * * * *

The weather was warm enough that I decided to let my antelope hang for only one night, so I cut and wrapped it for the freezer on Monday evening after work. I listened to music as I worked, and off and on I had memories of my silent observation of the white pickup out in the far-flung ranch country. In between, I had memories of Lynette Cole, with her trim figure, her even suntan, and her brown hair in a shag haircut that was popular at that time.

* * * * *

I did not see the Dodge pickup in the parking lot of the Buckhorn when I pulled in on Tuesday evening. I walked in through the side door, and in my first scan of the place, I did not find Tragg Tustin. His female companion, however, was standing behind the bar. As before, she was wearing a white blouse and black slacks. She moved toward me and took my order.

As she turned away, I took note of her features. She was of average height for a woman, with a thickening of her build that seemed normal for her age. I guessed her at somewhere between forty-five and fifty. I confirmed what I thought I had seen before, that she did not wear a wedding ring or have a light-colored area where one might be. When she brought my beer, I saw that her brown hair had a bit of grey near the temples. The shadows beneath her eyes seemed darker than before and uneven. I made myself not stare, but I stole more than one glance and thought I saw the vestige of a black eye on her left. I wondered if she was on the outs with Tustin and whether that was why he was not present.

"Three-fifty," she said.

I put a five-dollar bill on the bar. "Thanks."

When she brought my change, I pushed a dollar her way. She slid it out of sight.

"My name's Rick," I said.

She nodded. "I'm Rhonda."

"Typical weeknight?"

"Yeah."

"I saw you in here one night last week. Are you new here?"

"This is my second week."

"I don't go out much during the week. I live in the country. I've got a day job. I work at the USDA office. I don't like to stay out as much as I did when I was younger."

She raised her eyebrows and gave a matter-of-fact expression. "No kidding." She moved down the bar to tend to the other patrons.

I did not know how far I should try to take the conversation. If I waited until another night, I might come in and find Tustin taking up a bar stool, and I would miss my chance.

She came back when I was close to the bottom of my beer. "Another?"

I gave an appraising look, as if I had to think about it. "All right."

She set a full bottle in front of me, and I laid another five-dollar bill on the bar. She came back with my change, and I pushed a dollar her way.

She lingered out of courtesy, I thought. I did not find her unattractive, but I did not feel any spark.

"This is not a bad town," I said. "Everyone knows everything, like any other small town, but livin' in the country, I keep to myself."

"That's better."

"I've lived here for over twenty-five years. Had the same job all that time."

"Uh-huh."

It did not seem to me that she was matching anything I said with anything she had heard. I had the impression that she was just listening to one more customer tell his life story.

I said, "I thought I recognized the fellow who was sitting over there when I came in here last week." I motioned with my head toward the empty stool. "He was in town once before, several years back."

"Might have been."

"He was a backhoe operator."

Her face had a non-committal expression, but her eyebrows went up a little.

I smiled. "I don't mean to be personal, but I gathered that you knew each other."

She gave a light shrug.

"So I didn't meant to be telling you something you already knew."

"He's lived in a few places more than once. It's his work. Right now he's working on the pipeline."

"Putting the big pieces in the ground."

"Something like that."

"I didn't mean to be inquisitive."

"It's all right."

I smiled again, as if I wouldn't mind getting next to her. "Everyone has a past. When he was in town before, he was with a girl named Lynette."

"He's never mentioned her."

I gave her kind of a leer and said, "I don't suppose you talk about your old boyfriends, either."

"No more than I have to."

I could tell she was on familiar ground now, jousting with customers who wanted to know what time she got off work. I said, "Lucky for me, I don't have any girl-friends, past or present, to talk about."

"I bet."

"Maybe one. My ex-wife. But that was a long time ago. She's the type who would leave me out of her obituary."

"People do that. Would you?"

"Leave her out? I don't think I would. I don't carry a grudge all that much."

"Some do, some don't."

"Reminds me of a joke. The little chicken asks his mom, 'Am I a people?' She says, 'No, you're a chicken.' He says, 'Was I born?' And she says, 'No, you were laid.' He says, 'Do people get laid?' And his mom says, 'Some do. Others are chicken.'"

Rhonda laughed. "I hadn't heard that one before."

I think a fellow could have stayed in that bar all night and not gotten anywhere with her. I also had the sense that she was not on perfect terms with the heavy equipment operator. I wondered if something had him more touchy than usual since he came back to this town. But I did not have any real interest in her, so I did not have a hard time leaving after my second beer.

* * * * *

After dredging my memory for a couple of days, I remembered a person who knew Lynette when she was in town. Her name was Susan. With a little effort, I re-called her last name. Moncrief. She had a second-hand store in a building that sat on a lot by itself and used to be the location for a carpet business. She was about my age or a little older, and she had been a good one for telling jokes in the bar.

I found her sitting in an armchair with a small poo-dle in her lap. She had not had a dainty build when she was younger, and she was more than full-figured now. She still had a sparkle in her eye.

I took off my hat and said, "Hi, Susan. I don't know if you remember me."

"Rick Lemoore."

"Well, bless your heart. It's good to see you. You look good."

"Save it. I know I look like an old wreck."

I smiled as I met her eyes. "You look fine."

She waved her hand. "I remember you all right. You always kept your place. Not everyone did. But I'm done with all that stuff now, and I don't imagine you came around for that. What can I help you with?"

"I'm not shopping for anything. I thought I might test your memory."

"That might be dangerous. What about?"

"As the song says, just someone I used to know."

She drew her brows together.

I said, "Do you remember a girl named Lynette Cole?"

"Oh, sure. We worked together waiting tables at the Wagon Wheel."

"That's what I thought."

"I remember her last name because she used to sing those lines from a song. 'I'm just an old chunk of coal, but I'll be a diamond some day.'"

"Oh, yeah. I remember that one. 'Gonna grow and glow till I'm so blue pure perfect.'" I lowered my voice. "She knew a fellow back then. Name of Tragg Tustin."

"That's right. They lived together for a little while."

I felt a spike inside me. "I didn't know that."

"Yeah, they lived together, and then she moved out. Took a room at the old motel on the west highway, across from where the Overland still is. It was a motel that rented rooms by the week, like the Overland does now."

"That's where she lived when I knew her. But she didn't seem to be done with him. He gave me some static, and then I didn't see her again. From what I understood, they left town together, which surprised me."

"Me, too. He came into the restaurant and said she wouldn't be back to work. They were busy packing. So I never saw her again, either."

"And never heard from her?"

"Nope."

I shook my head. "I just wonder. He's back in town, you know."

"No, I didn't. But I don't get around very much."

"He's with some other woman now, which doesn't surprise me. I wouldn't have expected Lynette to stay with him all that long anyway."

"Neither would I."

"And, of course, I always wonder what became of her. It seemed like things didn't really end between us."

"Oh, I see. So you think you'd like to see her again?"

"Depends. At least know what she's up to. I know it's a fool thing to do."

"That's for sure. There's no fool like an old fool." She paused. "Sorry. Sometimes I forget to hold my tongue."

"That's okay. I think you're right." I glanced around at the used clothing, kitchenware, table lamps, and assorted small furniture. "I'll come back again when I need something." I took her card from a little tray on the counter.

"You never know. I might have it. Take care, Rick."

"You, too, Susan. It's good to see you."

"Same here." She petted her poodle and had what I thought was a sympathetic look in her eyes. I didn't know how much of it was for Lynette and how much was for an old fool.

* * * * *

The cry of the sandhill cranes carried from high overhead. I had been stalking a small band of antelope and had peeped over a low hill to find only a bare sweep of grassland. I paused for a moment to enjoy the solitude. I leaned my head back and searched the sky until I saw the thin, stitch-like line of birds. They flew higher than geese, and their call was almost haunting—nice music for a fellow standing alone with a rifle slung over his shoulder in the gentle sunlight of mid-morning.

At least I had seen antelope. It was a good start for the weekend. I had a doe/fawn permit that was valid for the rest of October, so I felt no hurry, although the animals became harder to sneak up on as the season progressed.

I walked back to the pickup, put my gun in the rack, and finished my tour of the pasture. I came out at the gate where I had gone in. The next place where I had permission was about four miles away, on the main road north, so I settled into my drive.

I had not gone far when I saw a white speck in my rear-view mirror. The road went up and down, and the next time I saw the white vehicle, it was closer. I didn't like the feeling it gave me, but white was a common color, and I planned to turn off the road into a pasture anyway.

I caught another glimpse of the white pickup, larger now, as I pulled in at the barbed-wire gate. I got out, opened the gate and dragged it aside, drove through, and closed the gate behind me. I drove in about two hundred yards, cut my wheels to the left, and stopped. About a minute later, a white Dodge came into view. As it passed, I saw a patch of grey where the paint had peeled. The driver was wearing sunglasses but no cap, and he gave his head enough of a turn to see me.

My stomach felt queasy. I had no idea of whether Tustin had been following me or was just going on a drive as he had done the weekend before. I wondered if Rhonda had mentioned her conversation with me. It would have been good ammunition in an argument.

I drove on into the pasture and tried to forget about what went by on the main road. I had an antelope permit, more than one place to hunt, and good weather.

* * * * *

Dust was rising from the unpaved road as I rolled along to the next place I wanted to try. The sun had climbed to its high point, and the air was warm and still. I had the familiar feeling of being in the slow part of the day when fewer antelope were about and when getting up at five a.m. was catching up on me. I turned off the main road, went west a mile, and turned north again.

In less than a mile, I saw a white spot in the rear view. I did not think it was a coincidence. I stepped on the gas. I was sure I knew this country better than he did. I knew the places where deer and antelope hung out, I knew the places that had locked gates, and I knew of one place that had an open gate and a haystack about a quarter of a mile in.

I was careful not to drive too fast on this road because I knew how easy it was to slide on thin gravel, but I pushed it. I slowed enough to go down off the road, through the gate, and into the hayfield. I stepped on it when I was onto the two-track, and I pulled around in back of a large stack of rectangular bales of alfalfa. These were the big bales, about three feet square and seven feet long. I parked behind the middle of the stack. I could not see the road in either direction, which I thought was good, as he would not be able to see me.

I eased out of the cab, tossed my orange cap in through the open window, and walked to the north end of the stack. In less than a minute, I heard the rumble of tires on the washboard road, and I saw the white pickup going north with the driver looking straight ahead.

I let out a long breath and held up my hand. My index finger had a slight tremble. I was not afraid in any usual way. After all, I had a bolt-action .270 Savage with a scope, enough to keep anyone from coming close, but I didn't like the idea of having to use it even to intimidate someone. At the same time, I felt I had cause for worry. Once might be a coincidence, but a second time, and turning onto another road twice, looked deliberate to me.

The rest of the day felt ruined, as far as hunting went. At least I had him in front of me for the time being. I imagined he would drive north until he realized he had lost me, and then he would turn around. He might loiter to see if I came out of somewhere again. I decided to head back to town while I had the advantage.

* * * * *

After a day amidst dry grass and dull sage, the images of yellow leaves, green lawns, and red Nebraska flags gave the impression that most of life was normal and sociable. I wondered how much of an illusion that was. I drove through town and on out to my place. By the time I climbed out of my cab after the long drive, I was a bit stiff. I also still felt that I had something to worry about. The .270 was assuring in a general way, but it would be awkward in a close-up situation. I did not like the idea of having to defend myself with any kind of firearm, but I couldn't let myself be a fool—not that kind, anyway.

I went to my gun closet and took out the pale red cardboard box that held my Ruger Single-Six .22 pistol. It had been a gift from my wife when things were still good, and I had not fired it for a long time, maybe ten or fifteen years. It had a cylinder for regular .22 long rifle and a second cylinder for .22 magnum. I had shells for both, as I had a rifle in each of those calibers and used them both for practical purposes in the country.

The extra cylinder came in its own small white box, so I set it and the red one on my desk and sat down. My hands were steady as I took the pistol out of its box. It was clean and pretty, almost new, a western-style revolver with wooden grips and a six-inch barrel. I took the regular .22 cylinder out by pushing a small button and pulling out the pin that ran through the center of the cylinder. I opened the smaller box and took the .22 magnum cylinder out of its soft, dark red bag with a yellow drawstring. I put the cylinder into the pistol and secured it with the pin. I was conscious of being careful at every point, and I went on to put five .22 magnum shells into the cylinder.

I was still wearing my tan hunting vest, so I slipped the Ruger into a plain leather holster and put it in the large front pocket of my vest.

I looked around in the garage for a target, and I settled on an overripe, round, dark green watermelon a little smaller than a volleyball, remnants of my last picking before the frost at the end of September. I closed up my horse in the corral and took the watermelon down into a gully where I sight in my rifles and do any other practice shooting.

I set my target on one side of the gully and walked away from it about fifty feet. I raised the pistol, clicked back the hammer, and settled the square bead into the squared rear sight. The pistol made a loud bark, and I could not tell where the shot went. I bore down the second time as I leveled the bead into the notch and fired. The shot opened up the watermelon and flung large pieces on three sides.

I did not know how many of my remaining shots went through the target, as it is difficult to see if a bullet goes through slush. But I felt as if I was shooting all right, so I put the gun in its holster and let my horse out of the corral.

Inside the house, I poked the empty casings out of the cylinder and put in five new shells. I laid the pistol and holster on a stand near the front door and reminded myself to take it with me when I went hunting again in the morning. I was calm. I had made every movement with caution as I handled the gun that had sat in the closet for a long time. The little interlude had not been very eventful, but the moment when the bullet opened up the watermelon and exposed its dull, overripe inside had been interesting.

For many years, I had not been one to shoot for recreation, but I appreciated what a firearm could do. As I glanced at the pistol in its holster, I recalled the rough voice of a man in another bar with a gravel parking lot. He was bragging about a .38 he had in the glovebox outside. He called it "that thing that barks here and bites over there."

I shrugged. I was done with firearms for the day, so I could have a beer and watch the sun go down.

* * * * *

I kept an eye on the rear view all the way out to the antelope country the next morning. Any vehicle traveling at that hour would have the headlights on, and I saw none up to the time that I turned off at my first cross-road.

I drove east into the sunrise for two miles until I came to the far corner of a pasture on my left. The barbed-wire gate had a piece of hardwood like half a length of ax handle hanging from a chain with small, thick links. I used the lever to open the gate and then close it when I drove through. I rambled along the two-track that ran on a diagonal toward the first windmill. Within a few minutes, I was into the rolling landscape again.

I felt a relief at being out of sight from the road, but I could not put the white Dodge and its driver out of my mind. On one hand, I thought that if I had followed him, he had a right to follow me. On the other hand, I thought he was being more aggressive, and I did not have a clear idea of what his motives were. I thought I had over-played my hand with Rhonda, but I hadn't done any real hustling, much less touch her. He should be content to get in my face the next time he saw me in town. I had a hazy idea that something ran deeper, but I didn't need to be dreaming up melodramatic scenarios.

I stopped as I saw a shade of light color on my left. A buck and a doe antelope were pushing up onto their feet. I had noticed for years that antelope did not get up as early in the morning as deer did, and I did not know them to move around at night. This pair did not bolt and run, so I stopped the pickup. They took off at a trot, crossed the trail ahead of me, and angled away.

Now I was into antelope hunting, which as a general rule did not have much tension or pressure. It was if I was on a boat in the sea, except that I could stop and get out when I wanted.

Less than an hour later, I picked a doe out of a group of three. I was on one knee in the grass, three hundred yards from my vehicle, holding my rifle firm on my bipod with the little crossbuck at the top. I focused on the animal that gave me the clearest profile, and I dropped it clean with one shot. I dragged it into a low spot where I could clean it on the rack I set up on the back of my pickup. Everything was calm and uncomplicated again.

I went out the same gate I went in, as I had done the day before, but now I had a fresh, clean carcass in a pale muslin bag. I was done with antelope hunting, and it was not yet ten in the morning.

I do not know if some imp got into me, but I had no sense of foreboding when I came to the more traveled road that ran north and south. Rather than turn left toward town, I turned right.

I drove north for several miles, meeting a couple of vehicles with clean-looking people who looked as if they were on their way to church. I knew that some pastors gave services at more than one church, and so not all services were at eight or ten. Still, the sight of these people helped me remember how early in the day it was. I also met an older man with a drooping grey mustache, driving a large, dark Ford and pulling a silver-colored stock trailer.

I had a tune running through my head. I recognized it as "Color of the Blues," one of the Patty Loveless songs I had listened to the night before. I could remember Loretta Lynn singing it as well. "Blue might be the color of the blues." Sunlight poured into the cab as I drove on.

The corrugated metal shed came into view when I approached the intersection, and I began to feel anxious as I made the left turn. I told myself it was early in the day and I wouldn't spend but a couple of minutes here. Furthermore, I would take the trouble to turn around and park on the opposite side of the road, as I had done before.

I was nervous when I shut off the engine, but I was not afraid. I took the Ruger out of the holster and put the gun in my vest pocket. The day was not yet warm, so I had the window rolled up. I left it that way, with my rifle in the rack and the keys in the ignition, as I stepped out of the pickup and closed the door behind me.

I looked to each side as I crossed the road. Far to the east, a black Angus cow was standing in the middle of the road, shining in the sun. I recalled that the road went through patches of open range both ways, including the spot where the shed stood.

I paused for a second at the door. I expected to see an old tractor inside. I thought I had seen a tractor parked outside at some time or another in years past, an old Case or Massey-Ferguson, not the newer kind with a tall cab that would not have fit through the doorway. I lifted the hasp and rolled the left door aside about two feet.

The shed was empty. The open door let in enough light for me to see a dirt floor with an old oil stain in the middle. Along the base of the left wall, a couple of grimy oil filters sat next to a blue plastic anti-freeze container. I took a deep breath and walked in. A dusty fan belt hung on the left wall, and a dull yellow hydraulic cylinder leaned in the back corner. On the dirt floor near the middle of the back wall lay something that looked like a headlight. I decided to take a look at it before I left.

It turned out to be an old, round headlight, face down. I tipped it over with my foot, and as it settled into place, the light pouring in through the doorway changed.

I flinched and turned around to see the shadowy figure of a man with no cap. As he moved inside, his right hand moved by his hip, and the light showed on a length of galvanized one-inch pipe.

My hand went to my vest pocket.

"Don't move," he said. It was the first time I had heard his voice in twenty-four years, but it sounded the same—full of menace.

"Keep your distance," I said.

"Tell me." He continued walking forward as I pulled out the .22 magnum. He did not seem to recognize it until he reached the middle of the enclosed area, where the old oil stain colored the dirt. "Don't think you're going to use that," he said.

I have to give him credit for having nerve. As I was clicking back the hammer, he rushed me. Everything happened at once. He raised his arm and was coming down and around with the pipe when I jerked my shot and hit him in the arm. The blast of the pistol reverberated in the metal shed, and the man let out a howl such as I had heard only once before, when a horse on the highway was hit by a gravel truck.

Tustin dropped the pipe and clapped his left hand onto his bleeding forearm. He backed up to try to block the doorway, and at the same time he looked around for the pipe. Darting forward, he picked it up with his left hand, but as he stood up, he had to bend forward again and hold his right arm against his mid-section.

I kept the gun trained on him as I edged around and backed out of the shed. As I dashed for my pickup, I saw his white Dodge parked on the side of the road by the back corner of the shed, but I was in way too much of a hurry this time to see where the license plate was from.

* * * * *

I met Susan Moncrief for a drink in the Lariat later that week. She had a light beer with a silver label, the kind that George Strait helped make popular. I had my regular with a red label.

"And she was buried there all that time," Susan said. "What a son of a bitch."

"To say the least." I was getting misty, but I pushed through to say what I had to say. "She was a sweet girl, and she didn't deserve to die like that. Then to be stuck away in a dark and lonely place where nobody knew where she was." I swallowed to clear my swollen throat, and I found my voice again. "I know I still hunted in that area for a few years after she disappeared. I must have driven past that shed twenty times." I shook my head.

"You can't ever know," she said. "The world is full of sons of bitches. Too bad you didn't get him with your deer rifle. He'd be done for now."

"I thought of that afterwards. It's a good thing I didn't. I would have it on my conscience, and on top of that, it might have messed up my hunting privileges." I was speaking clearer now. "He's in the right place, though. And I think they've got a good case against him. Having a body makes all the difference."

"I hope he rots."

"So do I. If there's anything good about this, it's that he didn't get away with it."

"You can say that again."

Of course I didn't. All I could think of was a pretty girl long gone away. I clicked my bottle against Susan's and said, "Here's to the girl who never got to be a diamond."

BUCKSKIN TRAIL

Benson slowed his horse as they reached the crest of the grassy slope. The gap in the sandstone wall would give him a view of the swale below. He had his eyes tuned for a change in color, as he was sure the light and dark colors of a buckskin horse would stand out against the short prairie grass. He had hunted this very spot, and he knew that the tiny valley stayed green into early fall when the surrounding plains were turning dry.

Little by little, the grassy bottom below came into view, darker in the afternoon shade than on the far side, where sunlight fell. No horse appeared, nor any deer. Benson relaxed in the saddle as he rode over the small rim and headed down. He stopped his horse by reflex when he spotted a dark form in the grass below. He nudged the horse forward and braced himself. The afternoon was silent except for the soft thud of the horse's hooves as he confirmed the dark denim trousers, tobacco-colored coat, and light brown hair of a man. A dark hat lay a few feet away.

Benson stopped and swung down, bent forward, and knelt to be sure. The man was a total stranger, and he was dead. That was the end of horse hunting for the day.

* * * * *

Night had fallen by the time Benson returned with the deputy and a packhorse from town. Moonlight cast a faint shade on the deputy's lean features as he stood by the body. He said, "This might be a man named Warren Voyle. His wife reported him missing."

"I have an idea of where they live, but I don't know them. I'm sure I never saw him before. It's too bad."

"It is." After a moment, the deputy added, "She said he'd been looking for lost horses as well, two of them."

When they had the body loaded and tied down, the deputy said he could take it in by himself. Benson rode home in the moonlight, thinking of his own packhorse, whether he would find it, and what a small loss it was in comparison with the death of a loved one.

* * * * *

His search for the buckskin horse took him close to the Voyle homestead the following afternoon. Based on the deputy's comment about lost horses, he thought the woman might be able to tell him something. He headed for the small group of buildings.

As he rode into the yard, a horse whickered. He turned to see a single horse in the corral, a sorrel shining in the sunlight. Movement drew his attention to the house, where the door opened and a woman's form appeared in the shaded doorway.

He drew near and dismounted. Holding his reins behind him, he took off his hat.

The woman stepped into the light. She was not a wilted prairie flower in a sunbonnet and a dress made of flour sacks. Rather, she was dressed for riding. She wore a brown hat with a rounded crown and a short brim, a tan neck scarf, a brown vest over a cream-colored blouse, and a pair of brown pantaloons tucked into high, dark brown boots. He guessed her to be a few years younger than himself, maybe thirty-five. Her hand moved at her side, and her voice came out clear and steady.

"What do you want?"

"My name's Tag Benson, ma'am. I'm the one—"

"I know your name. I just got back from town."

"I'm sorry, ma'am. I was out looking for a lost horse yesterday, and I'm doing the same today. I was in the neighborhood, so I thought I would drop in. If there's anything I can do, I'd be glad to—"

"Thanks all the same." She kept her grey eyes on him as a slight breeze moved her auburn-colored hair.

"I didn't see a horse near him, so I imagine you might be missing one as well."

"Three. My husband went out to look for two of ours that disappeared."

"I could be on the lookout for yours as well."

"I'm not in need of any more help. I've told the deputy everything he asked."

"I see. Then I won't trouble you anymore."

"No trouble so far. And thanks."

Benson took his dismissal. "And the best to you, ma'am." He put on his hat, led his horse out a few steps, and mounted up. As he rode away, he kept himself from looking back.

* * * * *

Out on the trail again, he met up with a rider he knew from the McGill ranch. He couldn't remember the rider's name, but the young man was cheerful and full of talk.

"Oh, yeah. I heard about the dead man. Heard of horses missing here and there, too. They're out on the range between roundups, y'know. Easy pickin's, I guess. Fall roundup'll be startin' in mid-October, not far away." He spit to the side and went on. "As far as what's goin' on, there's a new owner at the White Swan ranch. Name of Marvin. I heard tell one of the hired men was said to be a *gunman*." He jutted his chin as he gave emphasis to the word. "Maybe you heard that, too. But there's always talk. For my part, I listen and I draw my own conclusions."

"Good way to be, and thanks for sharin' what you know."

* * * * *

The sun was warm on the side of his face as Benson rode through the pale grassland. He had an idea of where the White Swan ranch was located. He paused on the main trail where a thinner trail led to the left between two small piles of rocks. Tracks showed where a buggy or light wagon had passed through in the last day or two. On a hunch, he followed.

The trail led uphill into the afternoon sun. A large outcropping of rock sat on his right side where the trail went over the rise. As he drew even with the rocks, a man on a dark horse rode out and blocked the trail.

Benson stopped. The rider had a bulky appearance, with a thick upper body, a high, rounded back, and a short neck. He wore a brownish-black hat and vest and a dark grey shirt. His shadowed face was hard to make out. He turned his horse around so that he continued to block the trail but now at an angle with a brown holster and a dark-handled pistol in view.

"Where do you think you're goin'?" he asked.

A thickness in his throat caused Benson to swallow as he picked his words. "I'm looking for a lost horse. A buckskin. I use him for a packhorse."

The man took off his hat with his left hand and dragged his cuff across his forehead. The sunlight must have warmed him where he waited behind the rock. He had a bald head, a furrowed brow, and a nose on its way to being bulbous and purple. He put his hat on, covering the bullet head and shading his face.

"That's too bad. That you lost a horse. But you need to watch where you go when you're lookin' for it."

"I thought I'd—"

"This is the White Swan ranch, partner." The man brushed his hand across his leg below the tip of the holster. "You best git back on the main trail."

"Will do." Benson turned his horse around and watched his own shadow as he rode away.

* * * * *

Shadows stretched in the Voyle yard as late afternoon was giving way to evening. The woman stood near the corral with a pitchfork in her hands, and she watched Benson as he rode in. She took a few steps forward, then rested the pitchfork upright with the tip of the handle on the ground.

"What is it now?"

He dismounted and took off his hat. "I was out look-ing for my horse, and I heard that the White Swan ranch over west of here might have something shady going on. I went to take a look, and a bullying sort of fellow told me to stay away. I was going by here on my way home, so I thought I'd drop in and tell you what I know."

"I've already heard of them. And the bully."

"Oh."

"It sounds like a good place to find trouble. And I'm not looking for any."

"Well, I just thought I'd mention it."

She did not answer.

"They say the fellow's a gunman, and he looks like it."

After a few seconds, she said, "You seem to have good intentions, and I would guess you know how to take care of yourself, but I would suggest you not go to any trouble on my, or our, behalf."

He understood her to mean the loss of her horses as well as the death of her husband.

"I'm sorry to bother you, then." He put on his hat, turned his horse, and stepped aboard. As before, he did not look back.

* * * * *

His trail took him north of the White Swan and northwest of the area where he found the dead man two days before. The land was more spread out, and the grass was thinner. He had not ridden this far north in the two years he had lived in the area, and he understood it was sheep country. He had also heard of a woman they called the sheep queen, who kept to herself but knew of everything that happened in her part of the country. He imagined a slender shepherdess, as he had seen in illustrations on book covers and calendars, holding a crook-neck staff, in front of a vine-covered cottage with a herd of sheep around her. But he had heard that this sheep queen had been around for several years, so he pictured someone older, with flowing grey tresses and a wise face.

He followed a dirt path that angled northwest. After a couple of miles, he came to what he thought was the place. Down in a hollow, a small house and two long, low lambing sheds were built up against the hillside on the west. Not a tree or shrub grew in the yard, and the ground was bare.

At least a hundred sheep grazed on a small plain east of the headquarters. They were all faced in the same direction, as sheep tended to do, so he did not see their heads, only their dull, greyish coats in the fading light of late afternoon.

A bell rang from the direction of the yard. Focusing his attention, he saw the full figure of a person standing in the shadow in front of the nearer shed. He directed his horse that way.

The person seemed to grow larger. When he stopped within twenty yards and swung down, he faced a woman of about his height with a thick build. He walked forward. She was wearing drab grey work clothes that showed to be a short-sleeved dress with a shirt and a pair of pants underneath. She had a full head of brown hair, tied back in a braid, and a broad face that, because of its fullness, looked as if it had been pushed up from the bottom. Her complexion was weathered, but her brown eyes were quick. Her lips moved, as if for practice, and then she spoke.

"How do you do?"

"Well enough. I hope I'm not too far off the main road. I've been out all day lookin' for a lost horse. A buckskin."

She made a short, dry laughing sound. "Been a long time since I've had any horses around here. Seen 'em, though." She glanced at Benson's grey. "Looks like he could use a drink."

"I imagine he could."

"Over here." She led the way with her arms at her side and her rounded stomach out front. She stopped at a low water trough and pointed at it. "Here it is. No charge." She made the laughing sound again, like a fizz.

"Thanks." Closer now, he saw the grainy texture of her face and the sparse, dark hairs on her upper lip. "My name's Tag Benson," he said. "I've got a homestead down southeast of here."

"I know the area. They let out a few sections for claims about ten years ago. You been there that long?"

"No. I've been there but a couple of years. I bought someone else's place. I'm getting to know my way around."

"This is a ways out. Heh-heh. But you know that."

"About as far as I'll go today, I think. I should be heading back."

"Gets colder here, as soon as the sun goes down. You can feel it already."

He shivered. His body temperature had gone down since he had quit moving and now stood in the shade. "I can."

"I should give you a cup of hot cider before you start back."

"Oh, no. I wouldn't want you to go to any trouble."

"Nothing of the sort. It won't take but a couple of minutes, and you can tell me about your lost horse."

Woodsmoke wafted from the stovepipe as Benson stood in the shady yard next to his horse. He had been waiting for more than a couple of minutes. He untied his jacket from the back of the saddle and put it on. The sheep lady brought out two chairs, one after another, and bid him take a seat. He did so, after tying his horse at the hitching rail.

The hostess brought out two large crockery mugs with steam hovering over the contents of each. She handed a mug to her visitor and sat down. She let out a huffing breath and said, "So it's a buckskin."

"Yes, it is." Benson took a sip. The cider was warm, not hot. He was thirsty, as he had been sparing of his canteen and had chosen not to drink out of the sheep trough. He drank about half the mug. "I use him as a packhorse, but you can't tell the difference when they're running loose. And he's all right as a saddle horse." The cider had a sweet taste that made him want to drink more.

"How long's he been missing?"

"About three days. Going on four." He drank the rest of his cider.

"Hum. You're done already. Let me get you some more."

"Please don't bother."

"It's no bother. And I want to tell you what I know about horses out here." She took his cup and went inside.

Benson felt relaxed. The shadows were stretching. Somewhere out on the pasture, the bell of a sheep tinkled.

The hostess put the mug in his hands and sat down. "By the way, my name is Moira O'Malley. Don't know if you knew that."

"Moy-ra?"

"Either that or Mo-ra. Just not Myra. Anyway, people talk about me, I know that much. So I thought you might have heard of me. Cattlemen hate sheep, say they graze too close and cut up the roots of the grass with their feet. Well, I'll tell you. Horses are worse, the way they tear up the ground. Put 'em in a pasture, and they'll cut a hundred different trails through it."

Benson took a drink. It was as good as the first one.

"That's horses for you. And the men that run 'em, they've got their trails. Not hard to follow."

"Run 'em?" His eyes felt heavy, and his voice sounded as if it came from someone sitting next to him. But there was no one there but him and the sheep queen.

"Yeah. Run 'em. Mostly at night. There's a trail I know of that's got nothin' but horse tracks."

The sheep queen was standing in front of him, leaning close. Her face was round and shining. He thought she said, "Sons a bitchin' horse thieves," but he might have said it himself.

* * * * *

He came to consciousness beneath a mound of blankets. He moved to one side and another and felt himself. He was wearing his clothes. At least he was not naked as a worm. For a minute, he thought he was in the other place, in Denver, where he had drunk too much brandy punch. But he was here. He remembered now. He rolled over with his eyes open and saw the sheep queen in front of a cast-iron kitchen stove. The clank of a skillet on the stove top had brought him to the surface.

The large woman turned toward him and smiled. "You're awake. Well, good. You need to take on some food. And don't worry. You didn't do anything. You passed out too soon."

His mouth was dry and his head throbbed as he huddled beneath the blankets. He could not just roll over. He had to face her, but he could not make himself speak.

"You think I drugged your posset, but I didn't."

"What's a posset?"

"A hot drink for a cold night."

"Oh."

"I didn't. You said you hadn't eaten all day. I think the sugar went to your head."

"I feel like hell now, like I drank whiskey and rum and brandy all together."

"You'll get over it. You need to get some food in you."

He felt wretched, but he knew he needed food. He rolled out of bed, pulled on his boots, and made his way to the table. A plate of fried potatoes and bacon appeared in front of him as he stared at the table.

"Coffee?"

"Please."

She set a crockery mug of coffee next to his plate. "I don't know how much you remember from last night."

He shook his head. "Nothing after the first drink."

"We were talking about horse thieves, and I was telling you about one of their trails."

"I think I remember some of that."

"Then I'll tell you again. Out east of here, to the north of where you say you found the dead man—"

Benson flinched.

"—there's a rough patch of country called the Whinstone Breaks."

"Winston?"

"No. Whin-stone. People hear it wrong the first time. Anyway, it's rough country, like I said. It's like a maze. But you can follow the horse tracks in, and they'll lead you to a place where they keep horses until they can move 'em on. A box canyon. I haven't been in there for years, since I could ride a horse, but from what I hear, it's still the same."

He nodded. "I should be able to find it."

"Just keep an eye out behind you. It's not a place for Sunday picnics."

"Thanks. I appreciate the information."

"Don't mention it. And I mean it. No need to tell anyone who let you in on it."

"Oh, no. I won't." He took a drink of coffee. "I'm sorry I passed out and made a burden of myself."

She fizzed with laughter. "Oh, you were all right."

He finished his meal, thanked her, and made his way out into the bright sunlight. She showed him to his horse, and in a short while he had the horse saddled and ready to go.

"Thanks again," he said.

Her face broadened with a smile. "You're welcome. Drop by any time."

He laughed and said, "You never know." He pulled himself up into the saddle and rode out of the yard with the sun in his eyes.

When he had ridden more than a mile and had two hills between himself and the shepherdess's cottage, he slid down from his horse and inspected himself. From the looks of things, it did not appear that he had done anything with the sheep queen, as she had said. At the same time, he did not believe what she said about not putting anything in his drink. He did not have an idea of why. Maybe she just liked company and wanted to keep a visitor for a little longer.

He shook his head. It would clear sooner or later. After making sure his jacket was tied snug to the back of his saddle, he took his gunbelt from the saddlebag, buckled it on, and set out for the Whinstone Breaks.

* * * * *

The horse trail led into rough country as the sheep queen had said, but the tracks appeared to be more than a couple of days old. Benson followed the trail into the maze. The sun had risen past mid-morning, so it did not give a clear orientation by itself, but the shadows it cast were helpful, and he kept an eye on his backtrail.

Draws and side canyons led away at various angles, where walls of sandstone and layered silt rose thirty feet or more. Vegetation was sparse, although in some places, patches of grass appeared on the canyon floor.

Game trails led into clefts too narrow for cows or horses, but cows had been here, as he could tell from old, dry cow pies.

He felt as if he was in the middle of the breaks when the rock walls became darker and the trail went through hard, fine-grained shale, unlike the porous rock he had seen in such abundance.

On the other side of the dark area, he came again into light-colored canyon walls with ochre stains, where spikes of harsh grass and tufts of goat beard grew on crumbly ledges. Higher up, pocks showed where he imagined birds had made their shelters.

The trail ended in a box canyon enclosed with a three-wire fence. The ground slanted up to the back of the canyon, where grass grew and a streak of green showed where water seeped or even flowed. Not one horse was present, and whoever had taken the last ones out had left the gate open.

Benson let out a long, tired breath. Heat bore down and reflected off the rock walls, and the air did not stir. He was sure there was more than one trail out of here, through one of the side canyons he had passed up, but he wasn't going to follow blind trails. Whatever horses had been here were long gone. His spirit sank at the thought of his buckskin running with the bunch.

He clucked to his horse and started back. He did not think the sheep queen had sent him on a wild goose chase, for horses had been in here, maybe in the last week. He needed to think about what he was going to do next. The first thing was to get out of here.

He rode through the stretch of dark shale and into the more familiar bluffs of sandstone and ancient dried mud. He had observed his backtrail many times, not only to see if someone was following but also to have a view of what the trail looked like going the other way. Even at that, there were aspects he did not recognize. It seemed as if more trails led off to either side. He told himself he needed to stay on course, and with the sun high on his right, he rode on.

The air felt lighter, and he estimated that the edge of the breaks lay about a quarter of a mile ahead. A bird flew up from a ledge on his left, and from beyond a partition of rock came the sound of crunching on gravel. The head of a dark horse surged into view, then the form of a man in a brownish-black hat and vest and high, rounded shoulders.

Benson used both hands to keep his horse under control, and so he found himself at a disadvantage when the man with the almost-purple nose leveled a six-shooter at him.

The man's voice came out coarse and scratchy. "Keep both your hands on the saddlehorn." He wagged the gun. "I told you once to watch where you go."

"I'm looking for my horse, and I don't think this is the White Swan."

"I don't like to be followed."

Benson frowned. The bullet-headed man must have been out in front of him on the way in, ducked off to the side, and picked a good place to wait for him on the way back.

The man cocked his pistol. "I don't tell someone twice."

The cry of a voice, a woman's voice, made him turn his head. "Stop!"

Benson saw his chance and did not wait. He pulled his gun, thumbed the hammer, and fired. The man in the dark vest curled, and his hat tumbled as his horse lurched.

The man fell to the ground, and the horse turned and lunged away, stirrups rattling, in the direction of open country. The woman on horseback had moved aside and let it pass. When she came into view, her riding outfit and auburn-colored hair were recognizable in the sunlight.

She did not ride forward, so he spurred his horse to walk around the fallen body and toward the woman on the sorrel horse.

"This is a dangerous place for a woman, ma'am."

"I have a name."

"Mrs. Voyle. I don't know your first name, and I don't think we're on those terms."

"I don't believe we are, but it's Isabel, for your information."

He took off his hat.

She scowled. "Oh, quit this stupid courtesy. You just shot a man."

Benson put on his hat. "He wanted to shoot me. He had his gun pointed and cocked. I can thank you for distracting him. Otherwise, you'd be talking to him, and I don't know for how long. He said he didn't like to be followed, and I believed him when he made ready to shoot me. He might have treated you the same way."

"You fool. I was trying to gather evidence on this man. I believed, and I still do, that he had something to do with the loss of our horses and the death of my husband. I told you I was aware of him. And now you've come in to botch it, and you've got something else you have to report."

"I hadn't thought that far ahead, but I'm sure I do. By the way, I've been into the middle of this place, where they keep the horses for a short while before they move them on. And there's nothing there. The danger isn't over, though. I can ride along with you to your place, if you'd like."

Her grey eyes held steady as the sun shone on her hair. "Leave me alone. I've had it with this place where men kill each other."

His face fell. "He would have shot me. What should I have done?"

She did not blink. "Just what you did."

Half the breath went out of him. He did not know what to say next.

"I'll leave this to you, then," she said. "Good day."

"I'll see what I can do."

She turned the sorrel horse and rode away.

He reined his horse around and nudged it so he could go back and observe the man on the ground. The man's bald head did not shine, as it was lying in the shade. His eyes were closed, and his mouth was clamped shut. He wasn't going anywhere.

The grey horse shifted. Benson looked up at the sun. He had enough time to ride to the White Swan ranch and see what else he could learn before he went to town.

* * * * *

The turnoff between the two little piles of stone looked as unassuming as it had before. Benson did not think he had to worry about being recognized. The only person who had seen him on his earlier visit was the bullet-headed gunman, and he was far away.

The trail led him over two hills and into a typical-looking ranch yard with a bunkhouse, a ranch house, and a barn with corrals. Downslope from the barn, on the left, a patch of box elder trees was shedding yellow leaves.

The footfalls of the horse sounded on the dry ground. The bunkhouse door opened, and a man with a wide-brimmed black hat stepped out. He was slender, below average height, and somewhere in his early twenties. His head went back as he stood in a kind of swagger. He had a holster slung on his hip with the handle of a revolver sticking out, and his hand hovered over the gun.

Benson dismounted and smiled.

"What do you need?" said the young man. He had a broad area above his upper lip, and he pushed his mouth out as he kept his beady eyes on the newcomer and the grey horse.

"Like to talk to the foreman."

The young man smirked and said, "I guess I'm as much of a foreman as anyone is, which is to say we don't have one. Everyone reports to the big boss. What do you want to talk to him about?"

"Lookin' fer work."

The young man motioned with his hat toward the ranch house. "He's over there. I'll show you to him."

Benson tied his horse and followed the hired man across the corner of the yard and up the steps onto the porch. With his head tipped back, the young man rapped on the door frame and went on in. Benson followed him through a front room separated into two parts by a square archway. The first part was like a sitting room with a sofa and a stuffed chair, and the second was like a waiting area with wooden armchairs. Beyond, a double door was flanked by two round columns painted glossy white. The doors looked expensive, with carved panels and a light-colored shiny varnish.

The young man rapped on a panel, waited for a voice, and opened the door. After a short exchange, he beckoned to his guest and went in, taking off his hat as he did.

Benson followed and took off his hat as he went through the doorway. He found himself facing a polished oak desk about five feet wide and three feet deep. On the other side stood a short man in a dark suit. The man was bald on top with a fringe of dark hair around the sides. He had calm brown eyes that roved over his visitor.

"This is Mr. Marvin," said the hired man.

"How do you do?" said Benson.

"Good afternoon. What's your name?"

"Tag Benson."

"Lane says you're looking for work."

"That's true. I am."

"What kind of work do you do?"

"Ranch work, sir. Just about any kind."

"Well, there's lots to do." The boss drew his eyebrows together and gave a narrow look. "Two things I don't like. One is someone who sits on his ass, and the other is someone who doesn't do what he's told."

"You won't have any trouble from me in that respect. I know how my bread is buttered."

"That's good." The man glanced at a pen he held between his hands. "Maybe I'll give you a try. I start a man at a dollar a day."

Benson nodded.

"Put your horse in the barn, and your gear in the bunkhouse."

The young man referred to as Lane said, "He doesn't have any gear."

The brown eyes fixed on the new man. "You don't?"

"Not right now, sir. Someone got off with my bag and bedroll. That's why I need work."

"You remind me of someone who worked for me before. And not for long." He looked at the pen in his hands and raised his eyes. "Are you broke?"

"Close to it. I spent my second-to-last dollar on grub yesterday."

"No one drinks on this ranch."

"I wouldn't think of it. I've worked at a lot of places like that."

"You look to me like you might need to dry out. Put your horse in the barn, and meet me in the bunkhouse." The boss turned to Lane. "Show him."

Outside, Lane said, "What he means is, you take your horse to the barn, unsaddle him there, and turn him into the corral. He'll go out to the pasture later. You'll ride company horses while you're here."

"I understand. And your name is Lane?"

"Gavin Lane."

"You already know my name."

"I heard what you said."

"I'll put my horse away."

"Sure. Then meet us in the bunkhouse, like Mr. Marvin said."

Benson led the grey horse to the barn, where he saw a regular assortment of saddles, bridles, halters, ropes, chains, and barnyard tools. He unsaddled the horse, led it out and around, and took it into the corral to let it go. While he was there, he gazed out to the horse pasture, where a dozen horses grazed. His pulse jumped when he saw a buckskin. As he walked to the far end of the corral for a better look, he felt a strange sense of detachment from the place he had come to. The buckskin had its head down and stood at a three-quarter profile, but Benson was sure it was his horse. He shook his head to bring himself back to the moment. He knew he had better not let anyone catch him gawking.

He took the bridle back to the barn and hung it on a peg above his saddle. His thoughts came fast. He had told Isabel Voyle that he would see what he could do, and now he was in the middle of a boiling pot. For all he knew, her horses were in the pasture as well. Even if he wanted to, he couldn't just take his buckskin horse and leave. He couldn't risk a confrontation of two against one. What he needed to do was to tell someone with legal authority and try to get back here before the horses were moved.

Inside the bunkhouse, he was surprised to see that the living area was smaller than he expected. The far end of the building was walled off with a partition and no door. The bunks were close together, and the mess table was sideways to the kitchen doorway. Lane sat at the table smoking a cigarette, and Marvin stood at the end. He was wearing a black gabardine overcoat and a matching hat with a short brim and a creased crown.

Benson did not know whether to sit or stand, but he interpreted that this was the place where the boss gave orders to the hired men, so he made no motion toward sitting down until he was told to do so. The other hired man had not taken off his hat, so Benson did not remove his.

Lane tapped his ash in a sardine can. "I think we're ready, Mr. Marvin."

The boss raised his chin and took in a breath. He spoke to Lane first. "I want you two to go out and look for Hedges. He should have been back by now." He turned to Benson. "Go with Lane. He'll pick out a horse for you."

Benson felt his heart beating, but he stilled himself by taking in a breath. "I need to get something to eat before I do anything. I haven't eaten all day, and I rode a long ways. I was hopin' to rest up and then hit it fresh tomorrow."

The boss's head made a slow turn. "You what?"

"I said I need to get something to eat. And I need to rest a little."

The boss's eyes widened, and his face flushed. "You don't tell me, mister. I already told you what to do."

Benson put on a pained expression. "What the hell, man? Can't you see I'm starvin'?"

A small spray came from the boss's mouth as he made a sound like "Puh." He said, "You can go saddle your horse just as fast as you unsaddled him. You get the hell off this ranch before you eat a bite of grub here. And don't lose any time doin' it."

Benson looked at the floor. He saw the boss's small black boots with inch-and-a-half heels. He raised his eyes and saw the clean-shaven face and angry eyes. "All right. If that's the way you want it."

As he turned and walked away, Lane began to follow.

The boss said, "Wait here a minute, Lane."

Benson crossed the ranch yard under a wide sky. He knew he was playing a lone hand, and he hoped he could get away without a scrape. He found a halter in the barn, caught the grey horse in the corral, and led him to the barn.

He brushed the horse, laid on the double saddle blanket, swung the saddle up, and settled it into place. He reached under the horse for the cinch and was drawing it up when he became aware of Lane near his right shoulder. Acting as if nothing was amiss, he drew the latigo through the cinch ring, up through the D ring, and back through the cinch ring. He looked over his shoulder, where Lane stood close enough to touch him with the wide brim of his black hat.

Benson spoke in a casual tone. "Why is the far end of the bunkhouse boarded up?"

"Because the roof is falling in on that end. What's it to you?"

"Nothin'. Just makin' pleasant conversation. What does Hedges look like?"

"You have a lot of questions."

"I saw a fella in town yesterday, drunk on his ass. About your size and age, but no hat and a full head of blond hair."

"He wasn't in town."

Benson reached down for the rear cinch, drew it up, and buckled it. As he reached in back of the saddle and snugged the leather strings that held his jacket in place, Lane moved closer. Benson had to pull his arm in close to his body to step back.

"Don't crowd me," he said.

"I don't like your questions."

"Leave me alone. I'm leavin' anyway."

Lane did not budge. "We don't like the way you come in here like a snoop. The boss wants to talk to you again."

"We already talked. Now don't crowd me."

Lane took half a step back and laid his hand on the butt of his pistol. Benson grabbed the young man by the shirt with both hands, pushed him back three steps, and slammed him into the wall. Tools rattled and fell, and the black hat spilled to the side. Benson slammed Lane again, then pulled him forward and tripped him. His plan was to follow Lane to the floor and take his gun, but Lane had his hand on the grip as he landed. He was squirming to get his arm free enough to draw.

Benson glanced to his side and saw a tool that had fallen to the floor. He recognized it as a wire stretcher, which had a handle like an ax, a thick metal band like a shackle around the head, and two links of chain leading to a clamp for the barbed wire. He reached for the tool, got both hands on it, and swung.

The heavy end caught Lane in the head and laid him out. His upraised hand with the pistol dropped.

Benson stood up and pulled in a breath. He collected his senses. Lane was done for. He wasn't going anywhere, just like Hedges. But the boss was not the Methodist preacher he looked like. The best way to get out of here was to act as if nothing had happened. If he tried to ride away on a gallop, he would have to go across the ranch yard, and either he or his horse could take a bullet.

He took off the halter and put on the bridle, looked himself over, and led the horse out into the sunlight.

Calm, he told himself. Marvin was coming out of the bunkhouse with the tails of his coat waving.

Steady. He led the horse forward a few paces, stopped to snug the cinch, and made ready to mount up. He had the reins in place and was about to put his foot in the stirrup when Marvin came close enough to speak.

"Where's Lane?"

"Gavin? He's in the barn."

"What's he doing?"

"He got caught short. He's covering his shoes."

The boss frowned. "What do you mean?"

"He's squatting with his pants down."

"In the barn? We don't do that here."

"I didn't know." Benson laid his hand on the saddle horn. "Well, so long, Mr. Marvin. No hard feelin's." He was putting the toe of his boot in the stirrup when Marvin said, "Stop."

Benson turned to see Marvin pointing a small, blue-black .38 at him.

"You come with me until I've talked to Lane."

"As you wish." Benson withdrew his foot and settled on the ground.

With the rein in his left hand, he pulled the horse around between him and the boss. When the horse was in the clear, Benson had his pistol drawn and found his target. Marvin was standing in the same place, moving his head to one side and the other and following with the small pistol. Benson jumped to his left as Marvin fired and missed. Benson shot him in the middle.

* * * * *

The grey horse and the buckskin looked on from the corral as Benson stirred a bucket of mud made from tan clay. He put on a pair of old, cracked leather gloves and began smearing the mud into the cracks of his shanty. A chilly wind was coming in from the northwest, and frost had been on the ground the last three mornings.

A neighing sound from the corral caused him to stand back from his work and look around. A woman was riding a sorrel horse into the yard. She was wearing a cap, overcoat, and pants all of a grey wool herringbone. Her boots were black, as were her gloves. She came to a stop about ten yards away. Her auburn-colored hair moved in the breeze.

"Good afternoon, Mrs. Voyle."

"And the same to you."

"Did you get everything straightened out?"

"If you mean my horses, yes. I recovered all three. I have sold them already."

"Oh, that's good."

"I need to thank you for your part in it."

He thought she said it in as few words as possible. "I was glad to be able to, and even gladder to come out of it in the clear."

She gave a perceptible nod. "The main reason I came by is to ask if I could hire you and your packhorse to take some of my things to town. I want to catch the train tomorrow."

"Are you leaving this country, then?"

"For the winter. I will decide whether to come back."

"If you want, I can keep an eye on your place for you."

"I hadn't thought of that."

He hefted the pail of mud as he met her grey eyes. "You know, to get along in this country, a person has got to do things well."

"That's what my husband said. Sometimes I think he was too sure of himself." Her eyes went away and came back. "Are you that way?"

"I don't think so."

"That's a good answer," she said.

About the Author

John D. Nesbitt is the author of more than forty books, including traditional westerns, crossover western mysteries, contemporary western fiction, retro/noir fiction, nonfiction, and poetry. He has won the Western Writers of America Spur Award four times—twice for paperback novel, once for short story, and once for poem. He has won the Western Fictioneers Peacemaker Award twice—once for novel and once for short story. He has been a finalist for the Spur Award twice, the Peacemaker four times, and the Will Rogers Medallion Award six times. He has also received two creative writing fellowships with the Wyoming Arts Council—once for fiction, once for nonfiction—and four awards for fiction with the Wyoming State Historical Society. Visit his website at www.johndnesbitt.com

JOHN NESBITT

"NESBITT IS A TRUE ARTIST."
—*WESTERN AMERICAN LITERATURE*

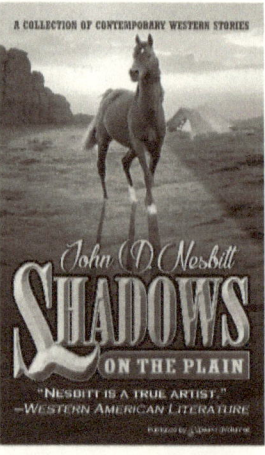

SPUR AWARD-WINNING AUTHOR
ROD MILLER

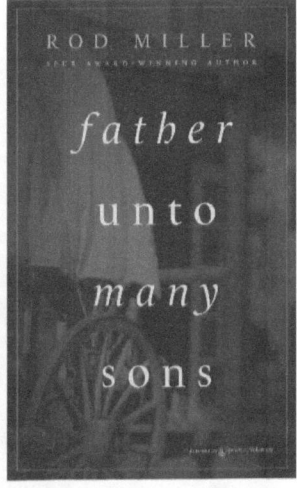

For more information
visit: www.SpeakingVolumes.us

GREG HUNT'S
ACTION/ADVENTURE WESTERNS

For more information
visit: www.SpeakingVolumes.us

www.ingramcontent.com/pod-product-compliance
Lightning Source LLC
Chambersburg PA
CBHW021450240626
47154CB00005B/1792